P9-CJD-014

Piggy Monday

A TALE ABOUT MANNERS

SUZANNE BLOOM

Albert Whitman & Company • Morton Grove, Illinois

To my friend and a wonderful teacher, Susan,

and to that sparkling class who inspired this tale.

—S. B.

Library of Congress Cataloging-in-Publication Data

Bloom, Suzanne.

Piggy Monday / written and illustrated by Suzanne Bloom.

p. cm.

Summary: The children in Mrs. Hubbub's class are so rude and thoughtless one day that they

turn into pigs and need the help of the Pig Lady to help them remember their manners.

ISBN 0-8075-6529-6 (hardcover)

[1. Etiquette — Fiction. 2. Schools — Fiction. 3. Pigs — Fiction.] I. Title.

PZ7.B6234 Pi 2001 [E] — dc 2001000805

Text and illustrations copyright © 2001 by Suzanne Bloom.

Published in 2001 by Albert Whitman & Company,

6340 Oakton Street, Morton Grove, Illinois 60053-2723.

Published simultaneously in Canada by General Publishing, Limited, Toronto.

All rights reserved. No part of this book may be reproduced or transmitted

in any form or by any means, electronic or mechanical, including photocopying,

recording, or by any information storage and retrieval system,

without permission in writing from the publisher. Printed in the United States of America.

10 9 8 7 6 5 4 3 2 1

The illustrations are rendered in gouache and colored pencil.

For more information about Albert Whitman & Company,

visit our web site at www.albertwhitman.com.

On Monday,

Mrs. Hubbub's class was getting out of line.
She told them to behave or they would all turn into swine.

No one paid attention. Mike began to tease.

No one shared, took turns, or helped, and nobody said "please."

The children still were wiggly, until they heard a wail:
Amanda took Melinda's seat, and then she grew a tail!

In music, it was noted,
Sara wouldn't sing the song.
She was busy whispering,
and then her ears grew long.

At playground as the teams picked sides,
they tried to leave Tom out.
Meanwhile Tommy picked his nose
and found he'd grown a snout.

Lunchtime was chaotic. Everyone was rude.
No one used their silverware, and George was throwing food.

Stevie used his sleeve when he was wiping off his face.
Suddenly, his hand was gone — a hoof was in its place.

At rest time Mrs. Hubbub said, "I've told you more than once. Good manners are important." But all she heard was grunts.

Nurse Judy took their temperatures and gave their tails a twist.
"It's no ordinary flu," she said. "We need a specialist!"

The secretaries knew just who, and in a snap they dialed her.
"Pig Lady, will you help us, please, before it gets much wilder?"

She came as fast as soda fizz and asked the principal where
she'd find the rude and rowdy class that doesn't care or share.

She lined them up and checked them out. She peered into their eyes, chucked their chinny-chin-chins and said, "This comes as no surprise.

"You've forgotten all your manners. In fact, you've gone hog-wild.
But together we can fix it." The piglets slowly smiled.

"Good manners are like magic. Everyone can learn
to treat each other with respect and be respected in return.

"Now let's get rid of those tails and ears. Blow your snouts and dry your tears.
It's really up to you, my dears: Can you remember your manners?"

"When I get picked on," Tommy said,
"it makes me feel so small.
So don't make fun of anyone.
Don't bully or name-call."

"We close our mouths," said Ashley,
"when we eat our food,
because it's just disgusting
to see what's being chewed!"

Kevin had a good idea:
"Take turns — the game goes faster.
If we fight and break the rules,
it's a big disaster."

"In the old days, when I wanted
something, I would just say 'gimme.'
Now I know that saying 'please'
is more polite," said Jimmy.

"You never play with me," Melinda said, "and it's no fun.
It feels so bad to be left out. I'd play with everyone."

Sara said, "We're sorry for ignoring you all day."
Then Amanda added, "Stay with us and play."

"I'll share my toys," said Keisha, "if you're careful and don't break them.
But ask me for permission first, before you go and take them."

Rebecca nodded, then she said, "It's up to us, I guess,
to put away the toys we use and clean up all our mess."

"I hold doors open," George announced, "and then say, 'After you.'
It really shocks the socks off people passing through."

"Excuse me, please! Excuse me, please!" said Jess. "I'd like to mention that when you say, 'Excuse me, please,' people pay attention."

"I get it!" Erica declared. "We hurt each other's feelings!
We were bossy, mean, and rude. That's why we started squealing."

"You've done it, dearies! I'm impressed. You've progressed from worst to best.
You thought your way through an awful mess. Yes. You recalled your manners."

Tails began to disappear. Ears shrank back to small.
Pig Lady shook each hand and said, "I'm so proud of you all."

Mrs. Hubbub thanked her as hooves turned back to toes.
The children and the principal were sad to see her go.

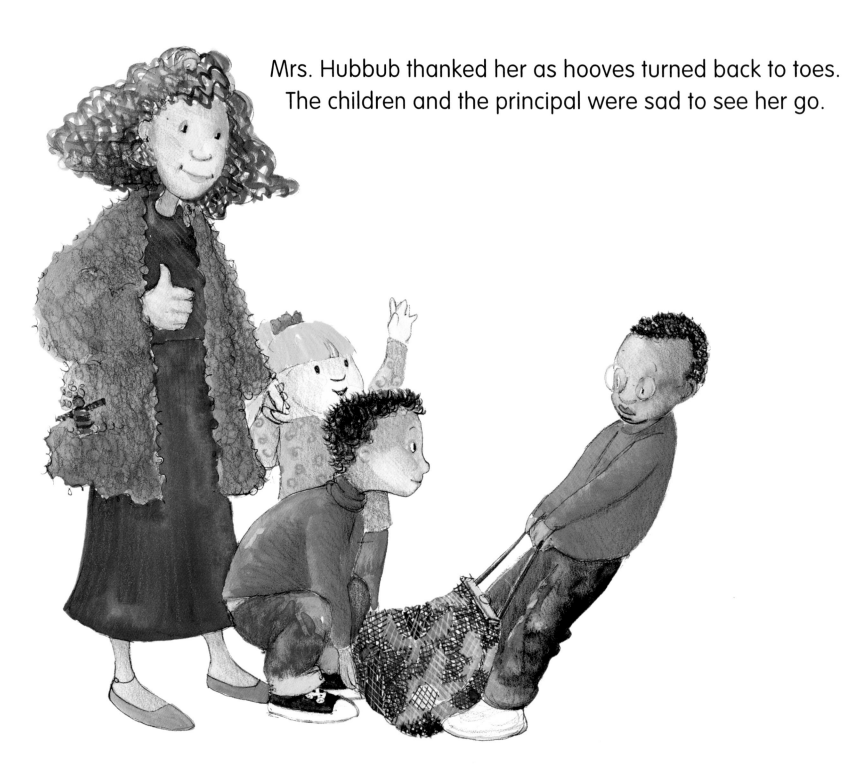

"I'm happy to have helped," she said. "And though I'd love to stay,
   there's another school nearby that needs me right away."

The class lined up for snack time. There was juice in every cup.
No one hogged the muffins, and everyone cleaned up.

"Excuse me," "please," and "thank you" were heard throughout the day.
Justin shared with Jesse, and Jake said, "Kev, let's play."

Whitney whispered, "Amber, you color very well."
And no one had a reason to shout "I'm gonna tell!"

The librarian was pleased to see the books put on the shelves.

In art class Mike and Erica did not paint themselves.

At bus time Mrs. Hubbub waved
to every boy and girl,
blew a kiss and said, "There goes
the best class in the world!"

Yes, manners are like magic:
whether you're small or big,
be sure to always use them,
so you won't become a pig.